Kelly's Diary

Written by Helen Orme

Illustrated by Seb Camagajevac

FULL FLIGHT

Titles in Full Flight 4

Badger Publishing Limited
15 Wedgwood Gate, Pin Green Industrial Estate,
Stevenage, Hertfordshire SG1 4SU
Telephone: 01438 356907. Fax: 01438 747015
www.badger-publishing.co.uk
enquiries@badger-publishing.co.uk

Kelly's Diary ISBN 1 84691 035 8
　　　　　　　ISBN 978-1-84691-035-7

Series Editor: Jonny Zucker
Publisher: David Jamieson
Commissioning Editor: Carrie Lewis
Editor: Paul Martin
Design: Fiona Grant
Illustration: Seb Camagajevac

Kelly's Diary

Contents

Sunday

Back to school tomorrow. Real pain! Why do we have to work when it's so good outside? Still – I get to see Simon again. Haven't seen him for a whole week!

And there's activity week. Mel and I are down for outdoor activities. We get to go to Wales to do canoeing, rock climbing and all sorts of good things. And Si is down for the same trip.

Bad news – Mrs James has said if we don't start behaving we won't go.

This is so unfair. There are people in our tutor group far worse than us!

Monday

With Simon for three lessons! He smiled at me!

The day wasn't too bad, but trying to be good is a strain. How are we going to keep it up for 4 weeks?

Did all my homework tonight! Even the maths which hasn't got to be in until Thursday.

There's a new girl in our tutor group. She thinks a lot of herself. The boys made a lot of fuss over her – even Si. They were all over her at lunch time, offering to show her where to go. I'd like to tell her where to go!

Mel said she looks like fun and we should be friends.

Tuesday

New girl – Alex (Who does she think she is!) is trying to be friendly. Mel is totally taken in by this. She said she could sit with us in art.

They were making so much noise that Mr Black had a go at me! He decided that as Mel was shrieking at the top of her voice, I must be too. So I got all the blame. Alex wasn't that funny anyway.

9

Saw Si at lunch time. Of course Alex was tagging along, so she started as soon as she saw him. If only she could see herself. Si was totally taken in by her. He didn't even smile at me.

I am never going to get anywhere with him while she's around.

Mel wanted us to walk home with Alex. She lives quite near to Mel. I didn't want to spend any more time with her than I had to, so I said I'd got to be back early and was going to catch the bus.

Mel went off with her.

Wednesday

Left my English homework behind today. What makes it worse was that I'd done it! Ms Wilson had a real go at me. Then she told Mrs James, so I got it in the neck at tutor time as well. Mrs J said she was fed up with me and I needed to start acting responsibly. She wouldn't believe it when I said I'd done it.

So now I've got to do extra English and hand both bits in tomorrow.

Mel was cross when I said I couldn't go out tonight, so I said, 'Okay then go out with Alex'.

Thursday

Mel was trying to be nice today – so was Alex. As if I care what she thinks. They had a great time last night and wanted to tell me all about it!

They met up with Si and his mates in the pizza place. Mel thinks Si fancies Alex.

What a surprise! He is so stupid he can't see what she's like.

I tried to talk to Mel at break. She kept saying Alex is fun and she wants her to hang around with us. So I told her exactly what Alex is like. How come I'm the only one who can see it?

Mel said I was just jealous because of Si. Then Alex sneaked up behind us. She must have heard what I was saying but she pretended she hadn't.

Friday

Alex was being really nasty about Ms Wilson at break time. She'd been messing about in English and Ms Wilson had told her off. The look Alex gave her! Anyway, I went off to maths even before the bell went.

When I got to the room, Mr Black and Mrs James were talking. Mrs James said, "I wish Alexandra Castle wasn't friends with Mel and Kelly. They are a bit noisy but they're not bad really!"

Mr Black said, "She's not doing them any good – they are being sillier than ever. I don't think the Head should have taken her. Not after what happened at her last school."

Maybe the teachers aren't as daft as I thought!

Sunday

I was too fed up to write yesterday. Went out with Mel. It was a good day until Alex arrived. Mel said she hadn't told her where we would be. Anyway, she found us. She was really dressed up. She took one look at my new skirt and top and asked if they'd come from the charity shop. Mel thought this was a great joke.

She spent the whole of the rest of the evening making sarky comments about my clothes and anything else she could think of. Then, when Mel went to the loo, Alex said Mel didn't want to be friends with me any more. She said I was no fun to be with, and I should go home. So I did.

Mel wanted to know why I'd gone home. When I said it was Alex's fault she got cross and told me to grow up.

I'm in trouble again. I don't know how it happened but I've lost my locker key. I didn't notice until I went to get my work for English. I went all through my bag but couldn't find it. So I was late for the lesson and hadn't got the work.

I got the spare key from Mrs James later but she told me off for not looking after my stuff.

And I shall have to pay for a new one if I don't find it.

Tuesday

I found the key. It was in the bottom of my bag after all. It's funny though, I thought I'd looked right through.

Maths was awful. Usually I like maths. Si is in my group and Alex isn't! Mel was okay. She's fine just as long as I don't say anything about Alex. What is it with that girl? Why does everybody think she's so wonderful?

Anyway, I opened my maths file and there was an old cigarette in my work. Of course, Si had to see, didn't he. He HATES smoking and goes on and on about how it's bad for you, and stupid, and childish and… all the rest.

He looked at me as if I am totally stupid. "When did you start?" he asked.

It's NOT mine. I don't smoke, I never have, but he wouldn't believe me.

Then Mr Black came over and he saw it. So I got sent to our Head of Year.

She wouldn't listen either. She said I must have been smoking in school. She's going to send a letter home and discuss my punishment with Mrs James.

Awful day in school again. Alex kept on about smoking. Mel had told her all about the fuss in maths. Mrs James saw me at the end of the day and said I couldn't go on the activities trip. She said they only wanted people who could be trusted.

That means there's a spare place so Alex asked if she could go. Mrs James said she'd have to discuss it.

Then I realised – it was Alex. She could easily have got my locker key, then dumped it back in my bag when she put the cigarette in there.

I'm going to have to do something. Problem is – what?

Thursday

School pretty bad. Si ignored me. When Mel came to sit by me in English, Alex pulled her away and made nasty comments.

But – things a lot better tonight!
Mel came round. She said she wanted
to talk about Alex. I said if she
couldn't think of anything better to
talk about she'd better go home.

Then she told me she didn't believe it
was my cigarette. She knows I don't
smoke, whatever anyone else says. I
started to tell her what I thought
about Alex but she'd worked it out too.

She said she'd seen Alex smoking – a lot! And she was fed up with her. She's so clingy and gets cross when Mel talks to anyone else. Mel said she's really sorry for not listening to me.

We are going to talk to Alex together.

We got Alex in the form room before tutor time. I said she was the one who'd put the cigarette in my bag, but she just laughed. Then Mel said she knew it was her and she'd better stop being nasty to me.

Alex lost it. She started shouting at the top of her voice.

She said that I'd been nasty to her from the start. She only wanted to be friends with Mel. But she didn't want her any more.

"You can keep your stupid friend," she said to Mel. Then she looked at me. She grinned nastily. "I don't need you any more. I'm going out with Simon. As from today!"

After that, we went to find Mrs James and told her everything. She says she'll think about it and see me on Monday.

Mel says that everything will be okay. I hope she's right.

Out with Mel this evening. We had a great time. We saw Alex – with Si. As we watched she took out a packet of cigarettes and lit one.

Then she offered the packet to Si.

So, it's now no mates for Alex.

As for me, I've got Mel back, and as far as Si goes – we'll see. I've not given up yet. But for now, life is sweet again.

x